Franklin and the Baby-sitter

From an episode of the animated TV series *Franklin* produced by Nelvana Limited, Neurones France s.a.r.l. and Neurones Luxembourg S.A.

Based on the *Franklin* books by Paulette Bourgeois and Brenda Clark.

TV tie-in adaptation written by Sharon Jennings and illustrated by Mark Koren, Alice Sinkner, Jelena Sisic, and Shelley Southern.

TV episode written by Nicola Barton.

Franklin is a trade mark of Kids Can Press Ltd.
Kids Can Press is a Nelvana company.
The character Franklin was created by Paulette Bourgeois and Brenda Clark.

ISBN 0-439-24431-5

12 11 10 9 8 7 6 5 4 3 2 1   2 3 4 5 6 7/0

Printed in the U.S.A.   23

First Scholastic printing, January 2002

Franklin and the Baby-sitter

SCHOLASTIC INC.

New York   Toronto   London   Auckland   Sydney

Mexico City   New Delhi   Hong Kong   Buenos Aires

FRANKLIN could count by twos and tie his
shoes. He was old enough to walk to Bear's house
alone and go to the ice cream store on his own.
But Franklin wasn't old enough to stay home all
by himself. When his parents went out, Granny
came to take care of him.

One afternoon, Franklin's parents were getting ready to go to a party. Franklin and Harriet were watching out the window.

"When's Granny going to get here?" Franklin asked. "I want to show her my new puzzle. And she promised to bring her fudge."

Just then the phone rang, and there was bad news. Granny was sick with a cold.

Franklin was very disappointed. So was his mother.

"I really wanted to go to that party," she sighed.

"We can still go," said Franklin's father. "We'll get a baby-sitter."

"I don't want a baby-sitter," complained Franklin. "I want Granny."

"Granny is a baby-sitter," replied his father.

"No, she isn't," answered Franklin. "Granny's Granny."

Franklin's mother started making phone calls.
Soon she announced that Mrs. Muskrat could baby-sit.

"Mrs. Muskrat?!" cried Franklin. "But she's never
taken care of us before. She won't know what to do.
She —"

"Franklin," replied his father. "You and Harriet like
Mrs. Muskrat. You'll have fun together."

"Hmph!" said Franklin.

Mrs. Muskrat arrived at five o'clock and settled in.

"If you need anything, here's the phone number," said Franklin's mother.

"Don't worry about us," said Mrs. Muskrat, shooing Franklin's parents out the door. "We'll be just fine. Won't we, Franklin?"

Franklin wasn't so sure.

Mrs. Muskrat turned to Franklin and Harriet. "Why don't you two keep me company while I start supper?"

"Can we do my puzzle?" Franklin asked.

"First thing after I make us a nice soup," replied Mrs. Muskrat.

Franklin frowned.

"Granny does puzzles first thing," he said.

It wasn't long before Mrs. Muskrat called Franklin and Harriet to the table. Franklin peered into his soup bowl.

"Are those brussels sprouts? I hate brussels sprouts!" he exclaimed.

"I'm sorry, Franklin," said Mrs. Muskrat. "I didn't know."

"Granny knows," Franklin muttered.

When supper was finished, Mrs. Muskrat asked
Franklin and Harriet what they would like for dessert.
"Granny always brings fudge," replied Franklin.
"Well, why don't we make some?" suggested
Mrs. Muskrat.
Franklin got out sugar and butter and cocoa.
Harriet got out pots and pans. Franklin cheered up
a bit as the sweet smell filled the air.

As soon as the fudge was ready, Mrs. Muskrat gave Franklin the first piece.

"Is it good?" she asked.

Franklin nodded. "But Granny always puts flies in her fudge," he said.

"Oh, dear," sighed Mrs. Muskrat. "I forgot how much you love flies."

"Granny never forgets," said Franklin.

As Mrs. Muskrat was cleaning up the kitchen, Franklin turned on the radio.

"Welcome to *Shadow Land*," said the announcer.

Mrs. Muskrat frowned.

"I think that show is a little too scary for a young turtle," she said.

"No, it isn't," declared Franklin.

Then he fibbed. "*Granny* lets me listen."

Mrs. Muskrat sighed.

Mrs. Muskrat left to put Harriet to bed. Franklin settled into his chair.

The show began with moans and sighs and eerie cries. Then came clanking and creaking, rustling and squeaking. Franklin looked around him. What was that shadow beside his bedroom door? What was that tapping noise in the corner?

Mrs. Muskrat found Franklin shivering and shaking in his chair. She turned off the radio and held him on her lap.

"I'm sorry, Mrs. Muskrat," Franklin whimpered. "Granny doesn't let me listen to *Shadow Land*. Now I'm too scared to go to sleep."

Franklin started to cry.

Mrs. Muskrat thought for a moment. Then she said, "If I were Granny, I'd let you stay up late and keep me company."

Franklin wiped his eyes.

"I think Granny would do that," he agreed.

When his parents came home, Franklin and
Mrs. Muskrat were sipping hot chocolate in front of
a glowing fire. They were on their second bowl of
popcorn and their third puzzle.

As Mrs. Muskrat was leaving, Franklin gave her a big hug.

"Granny's still my Granny," he told her. "But you're my favorite baby-sitter."